DC
SUPER-
PETS!™

Raintree is an imprint of Capstone Global Library Limited, a company incorporated in England
and Wales having its registered office at 264 Banbury Road, Oxford, OX2 7DY – Registered
company number: 6695582

www.raintree.co.uk
myorders@raintree.co.uk

Designed by Hilary Wacholz
Originated by Capstone Global Library Ltd

978 1 3982 3941 8 (hardback)
978 1 3982 4136 7 (paperback)

British Library Cataloguing in Publication Data
A full catalogue record for this book is available from the British Library.

Printed and bound in China.

COMET!

The Origin of Supergirl's Horse

by Steve Korté
illustrated by Art Baltazar
Supergirl based on characters created by Jerry Siegel and Joe Shuster
by special arrangement with the Jerry Siegel family

raintree
a Capstone company — publishers for children

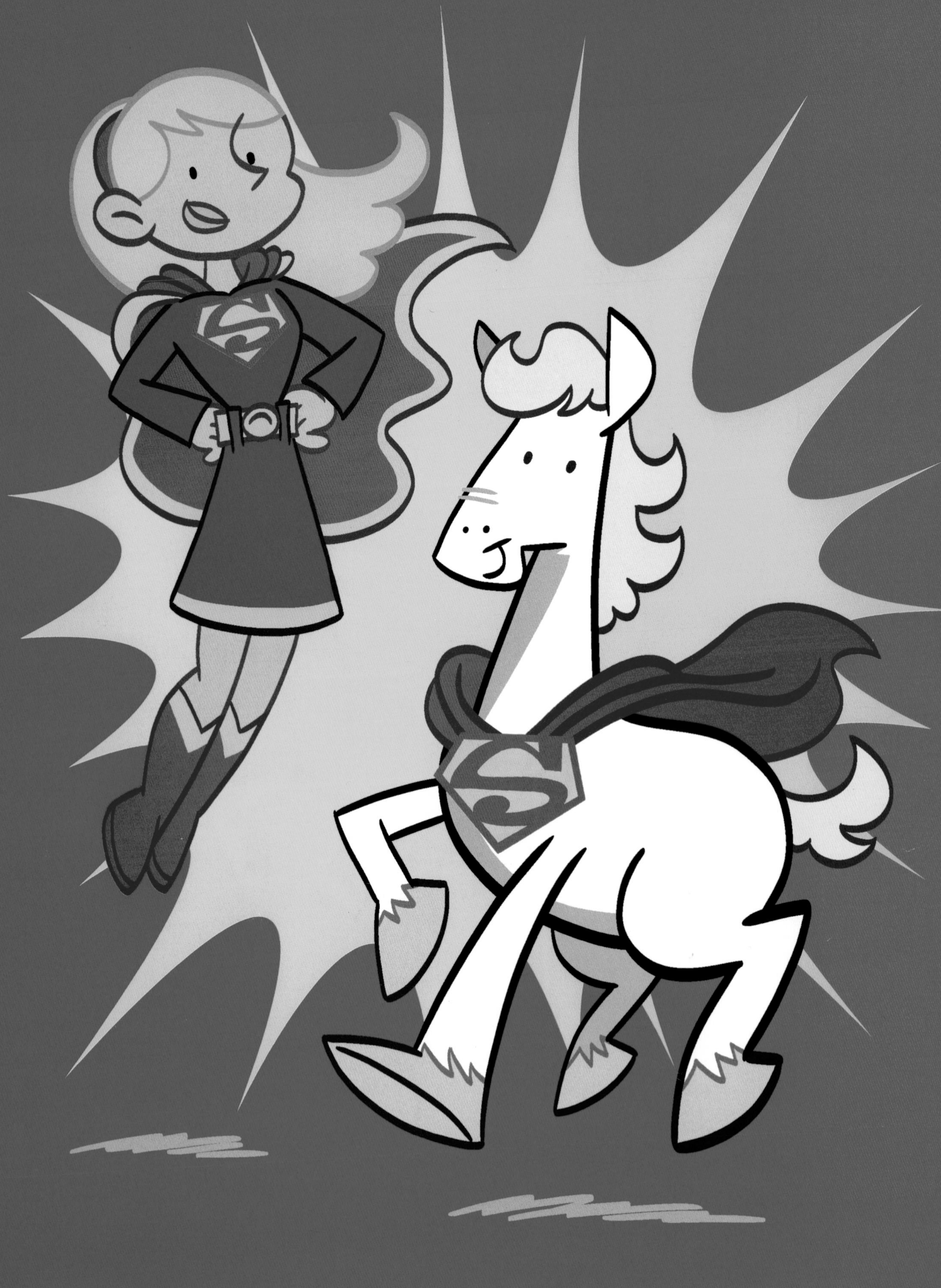

EVERY SUPER HERO NEEDS A
SUPER-PET!

Even Supergirl!
In this origin story, discover
how Comet the Super-Horse
became the Girl of Steel's
noble steed . . .

Just off the coast of Greece lies an enchanted island.

The island is ruled by a powerful witch called **Circe**. She lives in a giant castle where she prepares her magical spells.

Many amazing creatures live on Circe's island. One of these creatures is a centaur called Biron. Like all centaurs, **Biron is half human and half horse**.

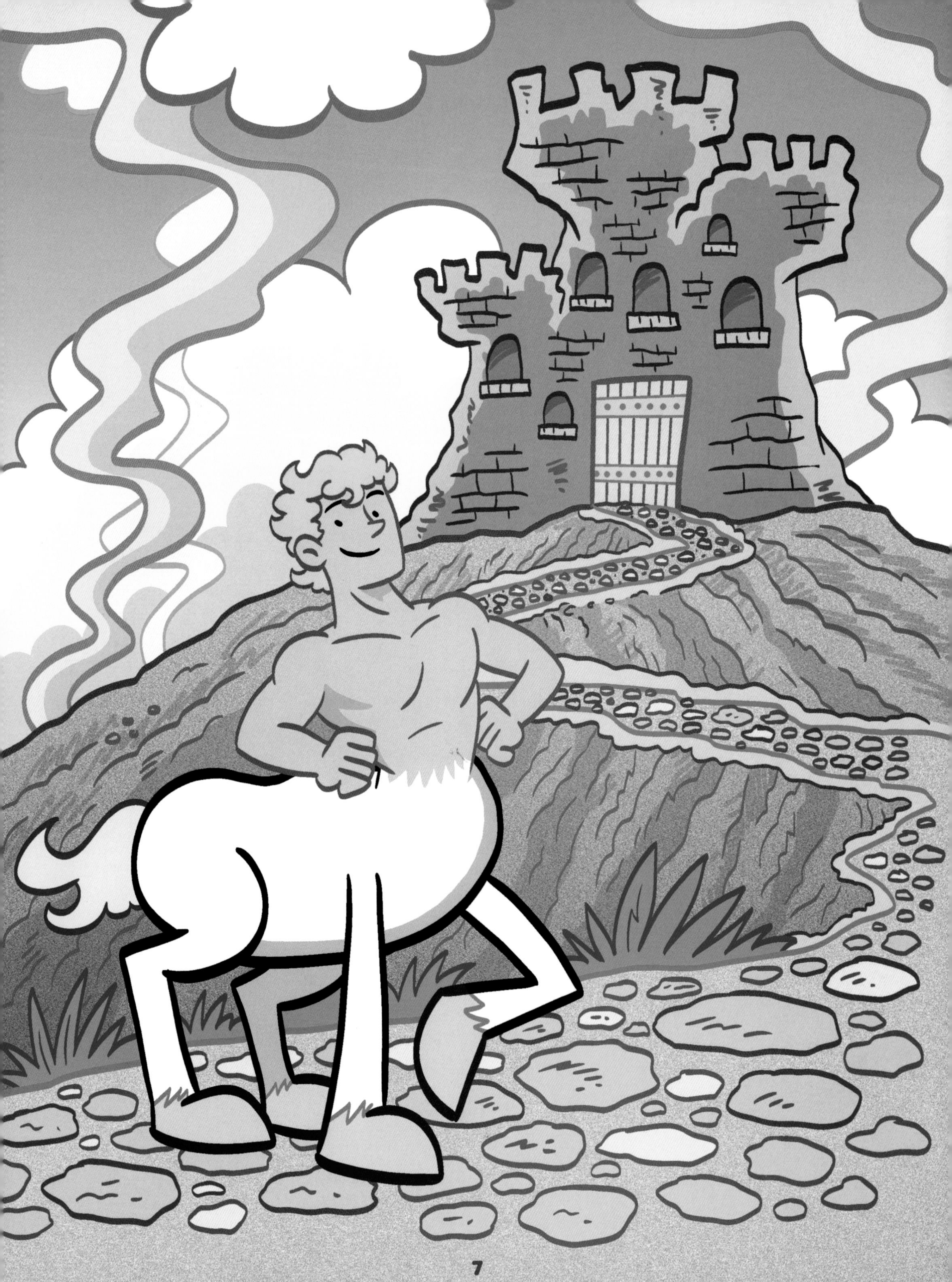

Biron sometimes spots Circe walking along the beach. He thinks she is the most beautiful woman he has ever seen.

Soon, Biron finds himself falling in love!

8

Biron wants to talk to the witch,
but deep down he knows he can't.

**"Circe could never fall in
love with a centaur,"** Biron says
to himself. He sadly walks away.

One day, Biron is walking near Circe's castle. He sees an **evil wizard** called Maldor leaning over the well where Circe gets her water.

Maldor is jealous of Circe's powers. The wizard reaches into his robes and pulls out a bottle of **poison**. He is about to pour the poison into the well!

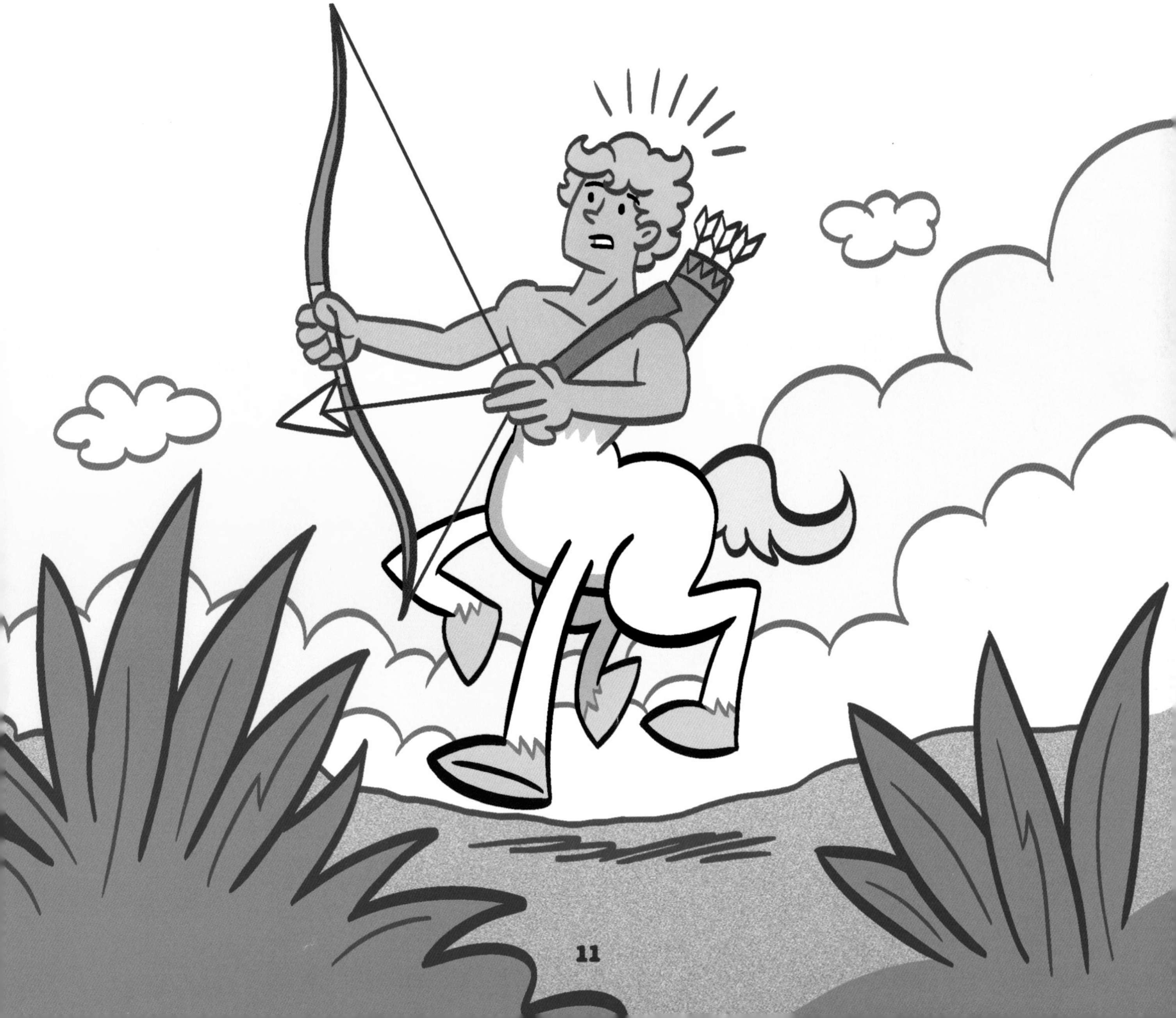

Biron draws back his bow and fires an arrow.

THWACK!

The sharp arrow bounces off the well, and the frightened wizard runs away.

Circe rushes out of her castle.

"You saved my life!" she says to Biron.

"In return, I will grant you any reward."

Biron smiles shyly and asks, **"Can you cast a spell to make me human?"**

Circe takes Biron into her castle. She points to a large pot that is filled with a hot, bubbling liquid.

"Drink this potion," she says.

Seconds after Biron swallows the liquid, he discovers that he is no longer a centaur. He is now a large, white horse!

"Something's gone wrong!" Circe cries. **"The spell didn't work!"**

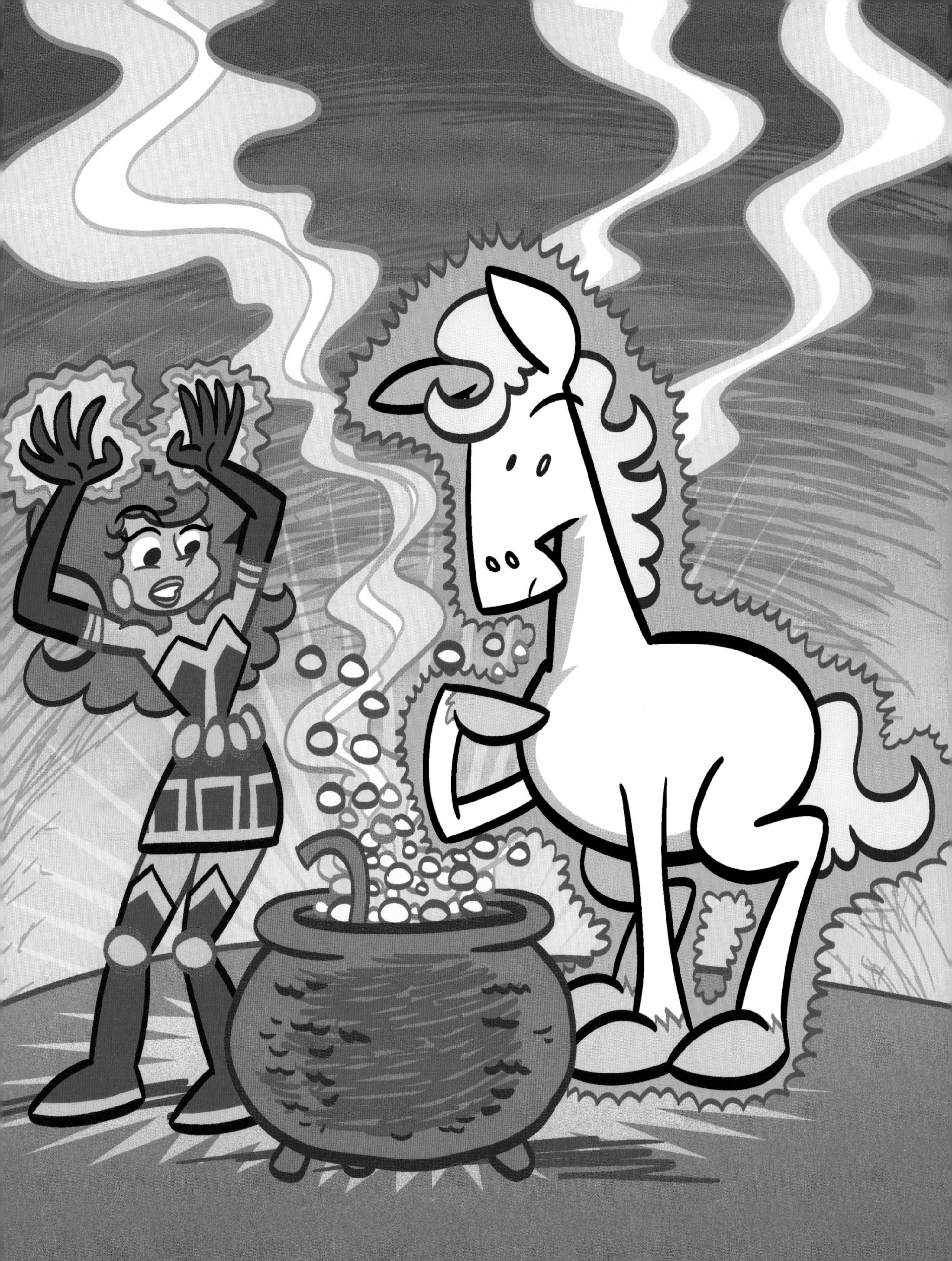

"I am so sorry," says Circe. "But after a spell has been made, **it can't be undone**."

Circe reaches out her hand to comfort Biron.

"I will make it up to you," she says. **"I'll give you many incredible superpowers**. You will have super-strength and the ability to fly. You will have super-vision, which lets you view things from far away. And you will now live forever."

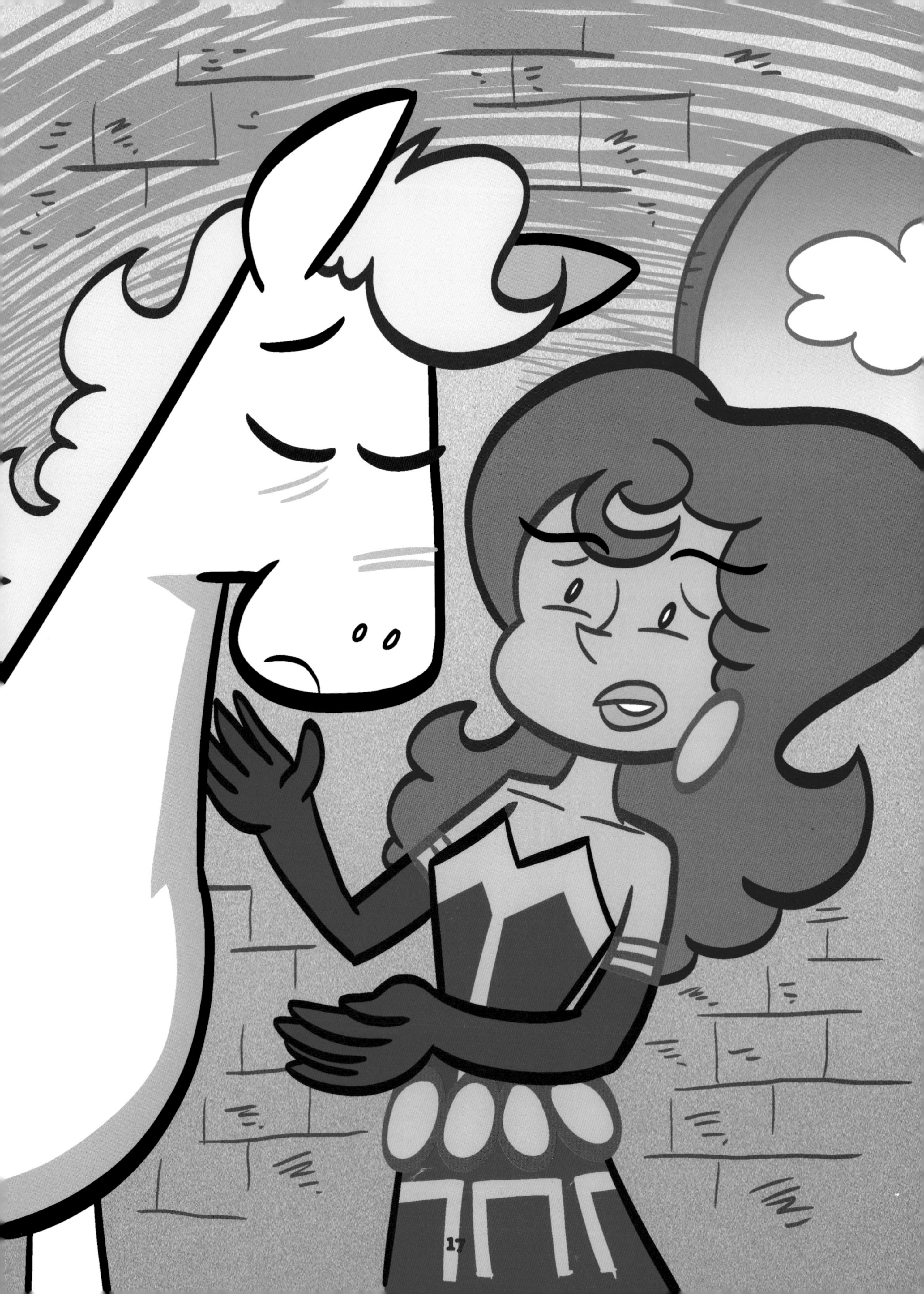

After Circe gives Biron the new powers, he sadly leaves her castle. He doesn't see angry Maldor sneaking up behind him.

Maldor casts a spell on Biron. It sends the startled horse flying into outer space!

THUD!

Biron lands on an asteroid millions of kilometres away from Earth.

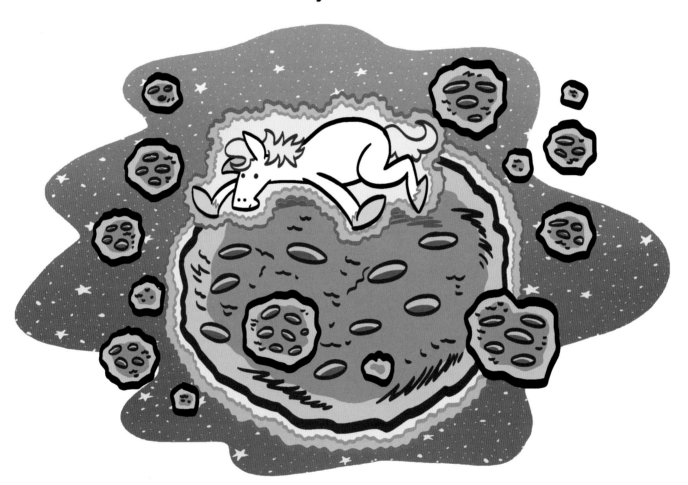

There Biron remains a prisoner.

He's surrounded by a magical force field that stops him escaping.

Hundreds of years pass, but then something amazing happens.

A planet called Krypton explodes in a galaxy not far from Biron.

Seconds after the blast, a rocket ship flies into space. The ship comes from Argo City, which was once part of the shattered planet.

Inside the ship is a young girl called **Kara Zor-El**. She is the last survivor of Argo City.

Kara's ship heads straight towards Biron's asteroid. Luckily, her rocket has lasers that can destroy anything that gets too close.

ZAAAAP!

The ship's lasers blast the magical
force field around Biron's asteroid.
The superpowered horse is free!

Biron flies after the rocket. When the ship
lands on Earth, Biron is right behind it.

Biron decides to stay on Earth.
He joins a herd of wild horses and uses
his super-vision to watch Kara grow up.

Earth's yellow sun gives Kara Zor-El
amazing superpowers, including
the power of flight.

Kara decides to use her powers to fight
crime and help others. She becomes the
mighty hero Supergirl.

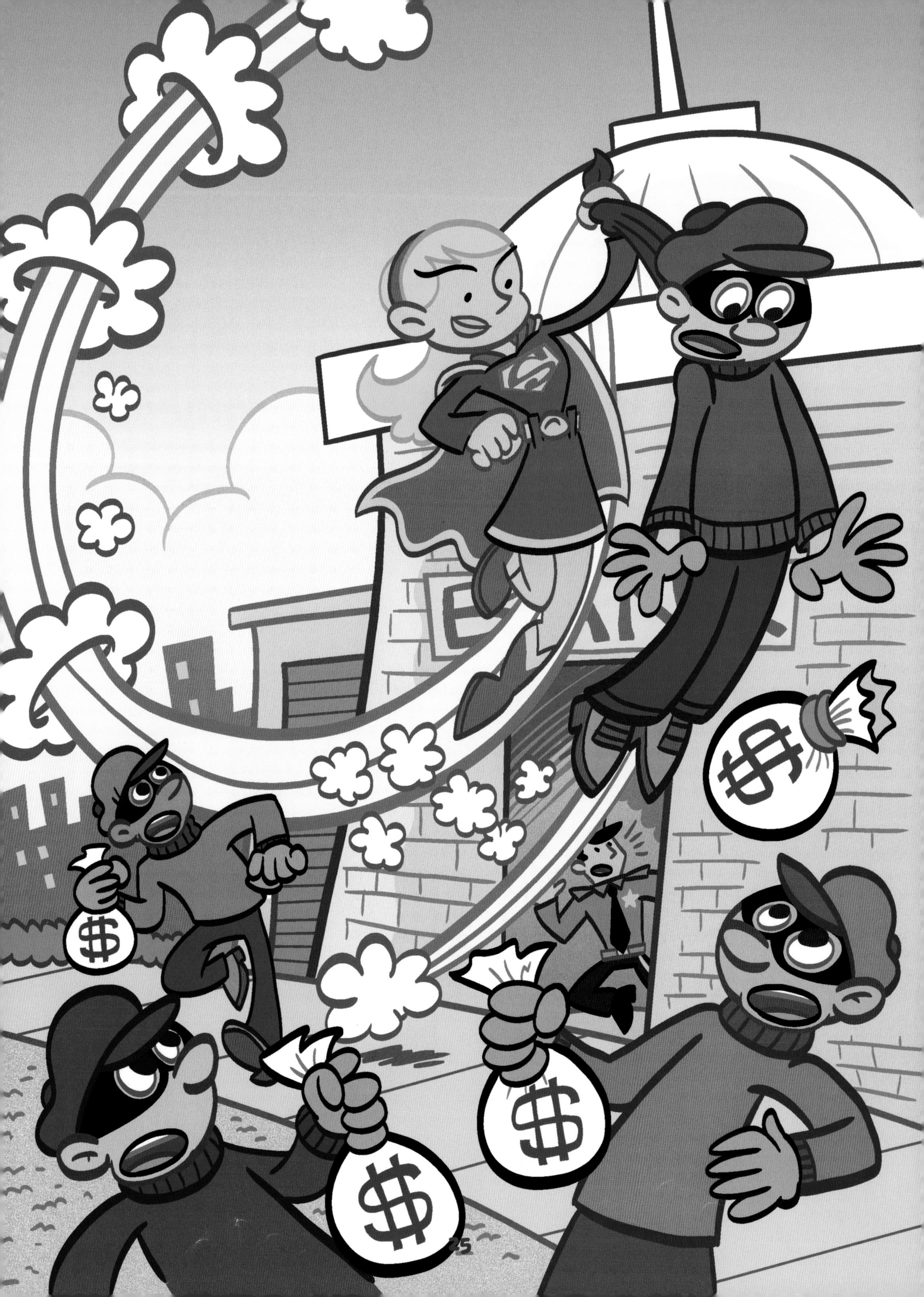

Biron watches Supergirl as she flies around the world.

"She's using her powers to help people," Biron says to himself. **"Maybe someday, I can join Supergirl on a mission."**

Until that day comes, Biron plans to

keep his powers a secret from others.

One day, Supergirl flies high above the city of Midvale. She waves to construction workers who are building the city's tallest skyscraper.

Suddenly, an alien spaceship appears in the sky!

A green laser fires from the ship. The laser blasts off the top of the unfinished building.

"Help! Help!" cry the workers.

Large chunks of the skyscraper tumble towards the ground.

Supergirl **zooms** to the rescue!

"I have to save the workers!"

she says to herself. "And I have

to stop the pieces of the building

hitting people down below!"

But there isn't enough time for
Supergirl to do both!

FWOOOSH!

Out of nowhere, **Biron swoops through the air!** He gathers up the pieces of the building in his mouth.

Supergirl is amazed to see a horse arrive like a comet from the sky. She lowers the construction workers to safety and then flies towards the alien spaceship.

33

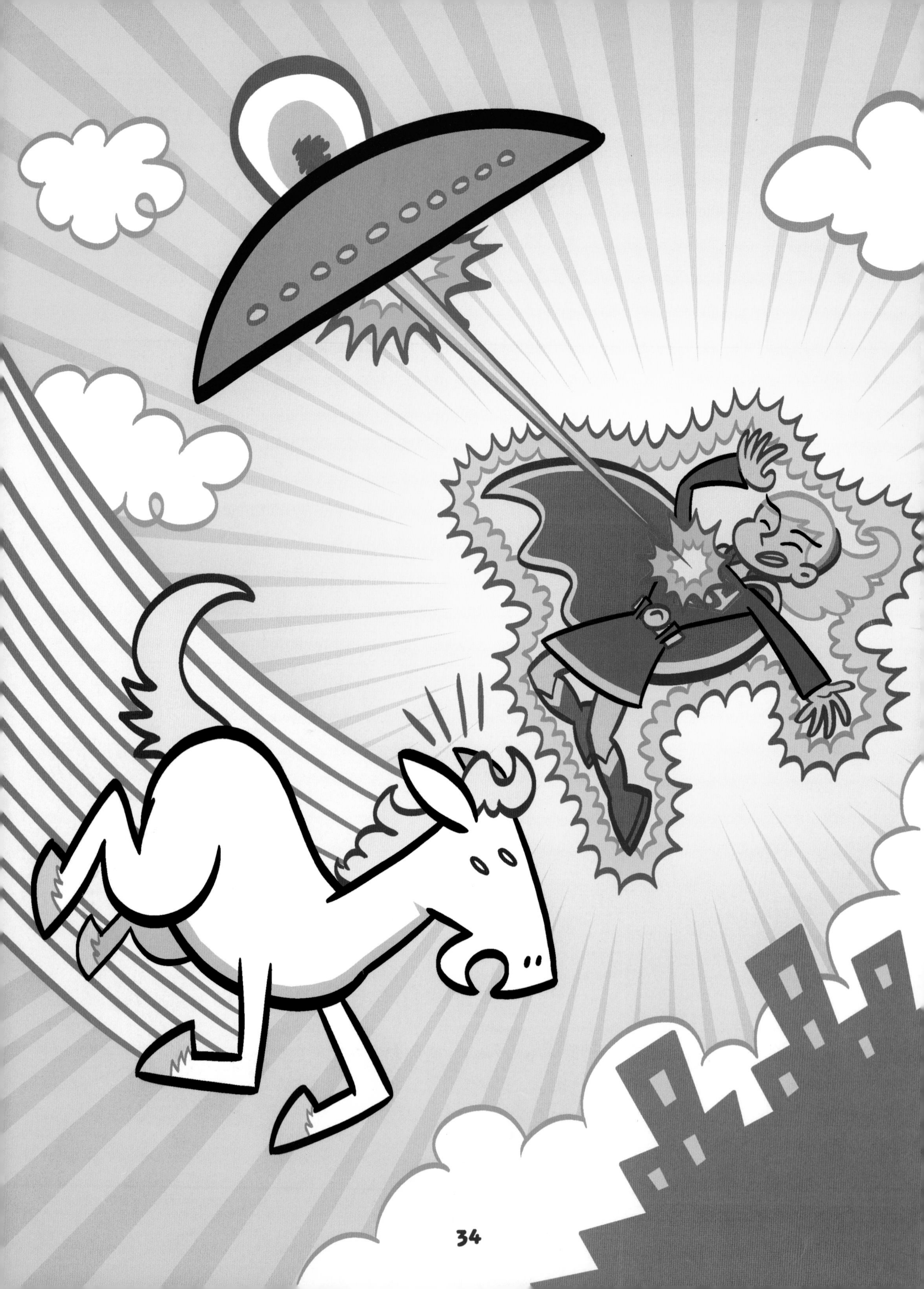

The ship blasts Supergirl with a ray of deadly green **Kryptonite**. It is the one substance that can weaken Supergirl!

Supergirl falls towards the ground.

Biron dives under Supergirl and carries her away from the green ray.

Because Biron is not from Krypton, **Kryptonite does not harm him.**

Supergirl recovers as Biron flies towards the spaceship.

Biron smashes his rear hooves against the ship.

The side of the spaceship breaks apart. Three pink aliens tumble out.

Supergirl and Biron grab the aliens and carry them to the ground.

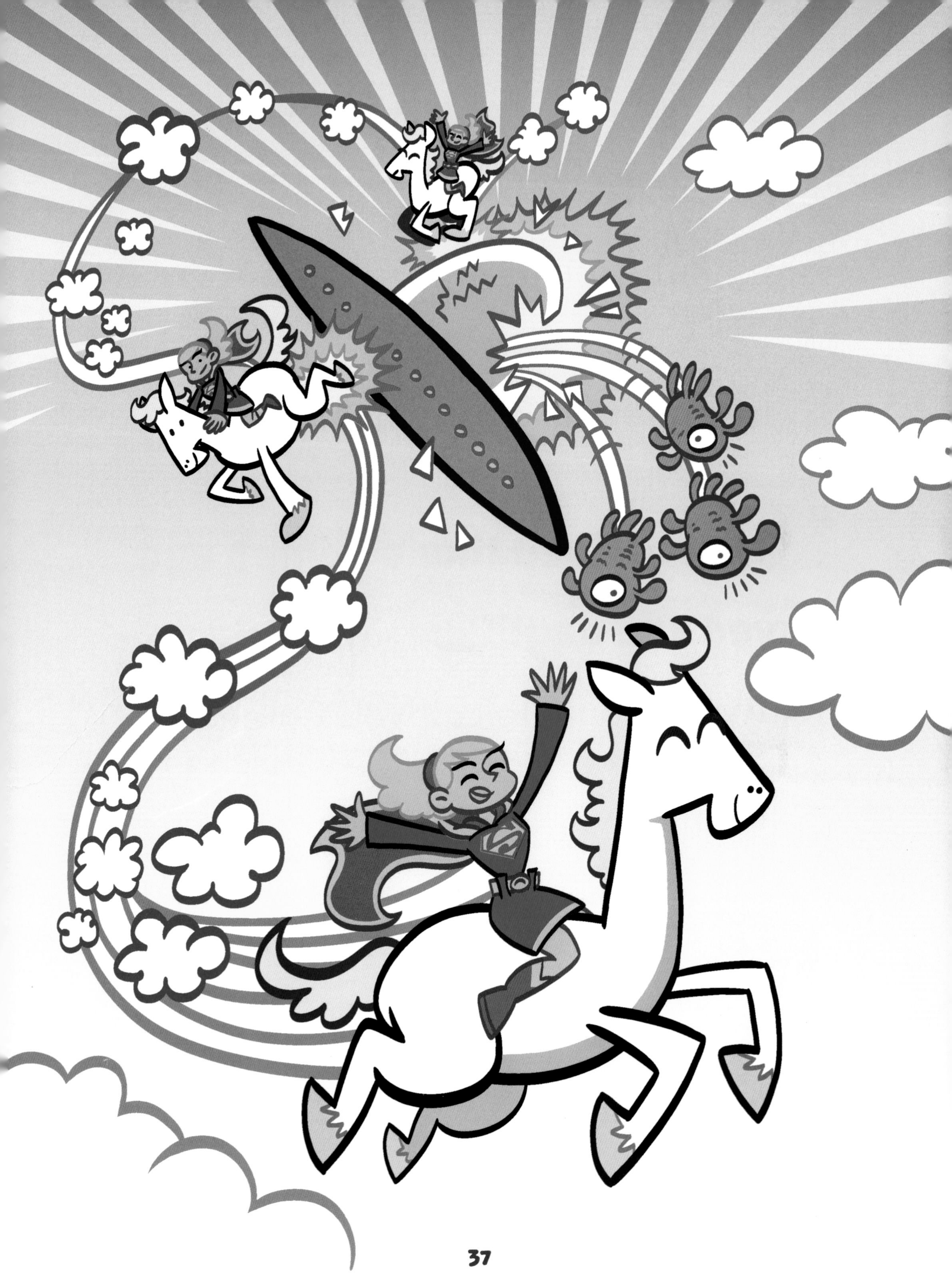

Supergirl blasts a steel bar with her heat vision. She bends the melted bar around the aliens to trap them.

Supergirl pats Biron's head.

"You arrived like a comet and saved the day!" she says. "If it's okay, I'm going to call you Comet."

The horse smiles in agreement and nuzzles against Supergirl's hand.

Supergirl makes a red cape for Comet and gives him an S-shield to wear around his neck.

The next day, the people of Midvale look up in the sky.

Flying high above are two Super Heroes! It's Supergirl and her new crime-fighting partner . . . **Comet the Super-Horse!**

COMET!

REAL NAME:
Biron

SPECIES:
Super-Horse

BIRTHPLACE:
Greece

HEIGHT:
1.9 metres

WEIGHT:
408 kilograms

**Super Hero Owner:
SUPERGIRL**

**HEAT &
X-RAY VISION**

SUPER-HEARING

**SUPER-
SMELL**

FLIGHT
This globe-trotter
zooms to wherever
help is needed.

S-SHIELD

**STRONG
TAIL**

SUPER-STRENGTH
Comet isn't horsing around.
His kick packs a major wallop!

**SUPER-
SPEED**
This Super-Horse
is always ready to
giddy-up and go!

HERO PET PALS!

BEPPO

Super Hero Owner:
SUPERMAN

SUPER-SQUIRREL

Super Hero Owner:
SUPERBOY

VILLAIN PET FOES!

GRYLL

Super-Villain Owner:
CIRCE

BIZARRO COMET

Super-Villain Owner:
BIZARRO

COMET JOKES!

Where does a horse live?
**In a neigh-
bourhood!**

When will a horse talk?
Whinny wants to!

What does a horse say
when she trips?
**I fell down, and I
can't giddy-up!**

GLOSSARY!

asteroid large rocky object that travels through outer space

centaur creature with the head and chest of a human and the body of a horse

comet ball of rock and ice that travels through outer space

enchanted put under a magic spell

force field wall made of energy that stops movement

laser thin, intense, high-energy beam of light

poison substance that can harm or kill someone

steed horse used or trained for riding

wizard person, usually a man, who has magical powers

READ THEM ALL!

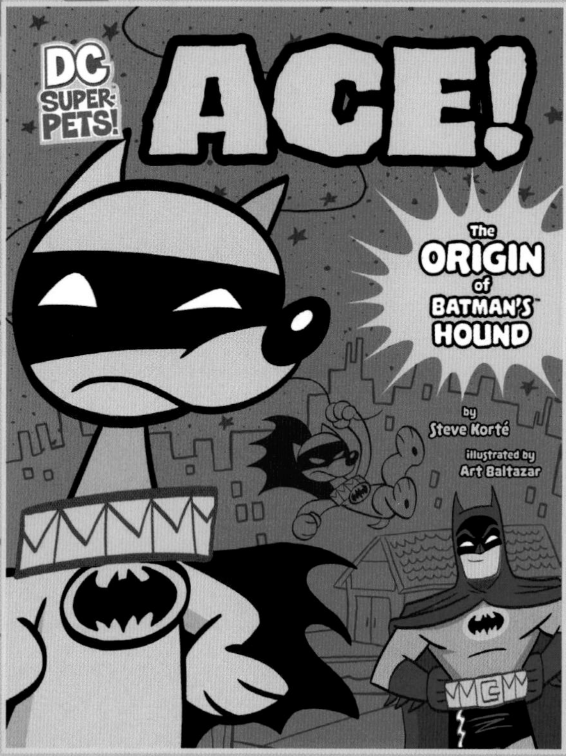
DC SUPER-PETS!
ACE!
The ORIGIN of BATMAN'S HOUND
by Steve Korté
illustrated by Art Baltazar

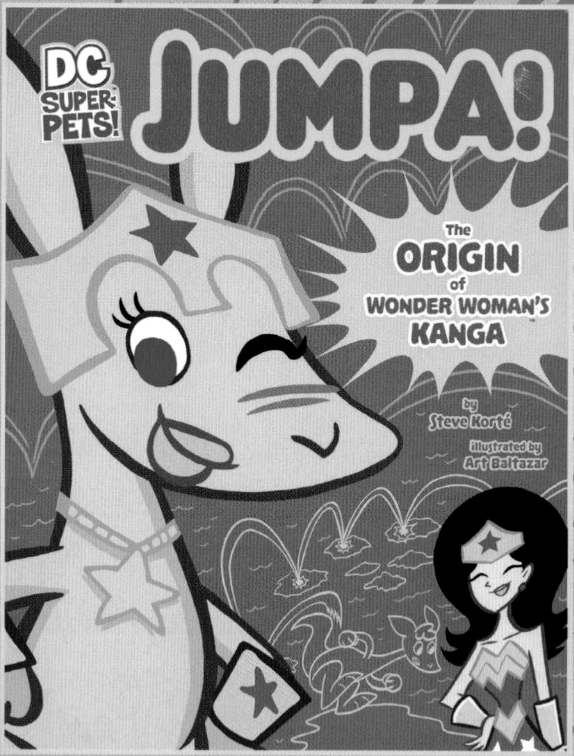
DC SUPER-PETS!
JUMPA!
The ORIGIN of WONDER WOMAN'S KANGA
by Steve Korté
illustrated by Art Baltazar

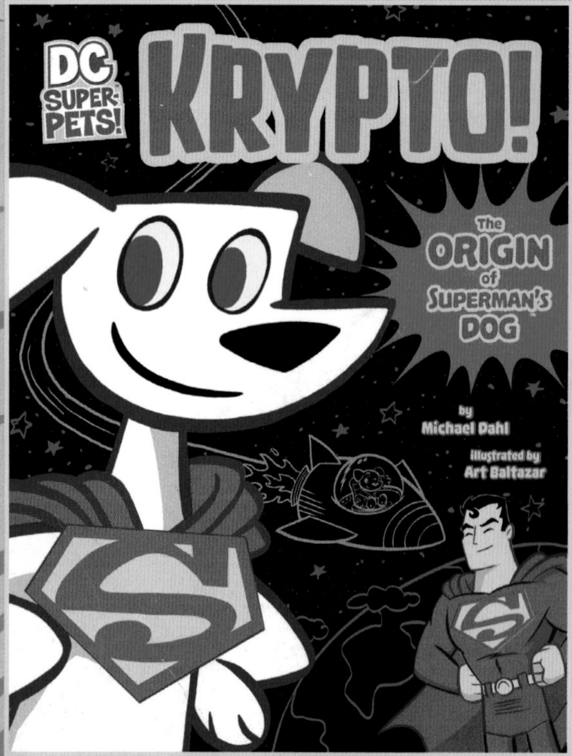
DC SUPER-PETS!
KRYPTO!
The ORIGIN of SUPERMAN'S DOG
by Michael Dahl
illustrated by Art Baltazar

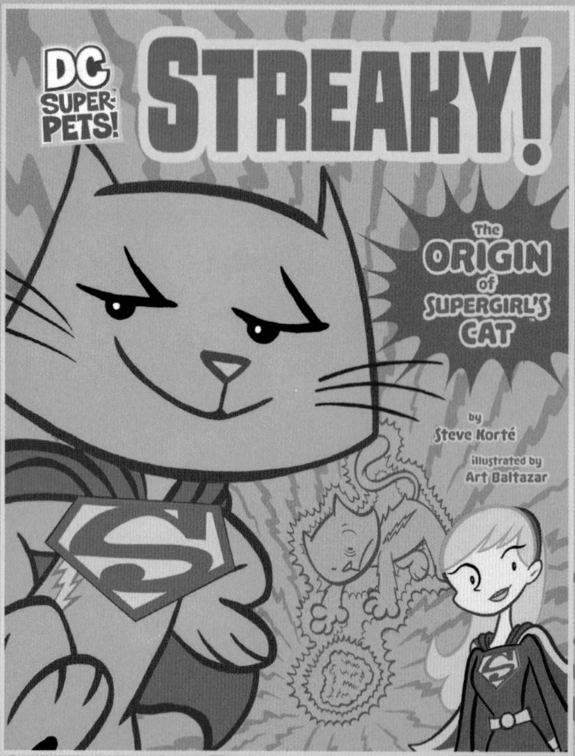
DC SUPER-PETS!
STREAKY!
The ORIGIN of SUPERGIRL'S CAT
by Steve Korté
illustrated by Art Baltazar

ONLY FROM raintree

AUTHOR!

Steve Korté is the author of many books for children and young adults. He worked at DC Comics for many years, editing more than 600 books about Superman, Batman, Wonder Woman and the other heroes and villains in the DC Universe. He lives in New York City with his husband, Bill, and their super-cat, Duke.

ILLUSTRATOR!

Famous cartoonist **Art Baltazar** is the creative force behind *The New York Times* best-selling, Eisner Award-winning DC Comics' Tiny Titans; co-writer for Billy Batson and the Magic of Shazam!, Young Justice, Green Lantern: The Animated Series (comic); and artist/co-writer for the awesome Tiny Titans/Little Archie crossover, Superman Family Adventures, Super Powers! and Itty Bitty Hellboy. Art is one of the founders of Aw Yeah Comics comic shop and the ongoing comic series. Aw yeah, living the dream! He stays at home and draws comics and never has to leave the house! He lives with his lovely wife, Rose, sons Sonny and Gordon, and daughter, Audrey! AW YEAH, MAN!